Time to Rhyme With Calico Cat

written and illustrated by Donald Charles

CHILDRENS PRESS, CHICAGO

for grit

Library of Congress Cataloging in Publication Data

Charles, Donald.
   Time to rhyme with Calico Cat.

   SUMMARY: Calico Cat and Shaggy Dog compose rhymes such as "There's a rose on my nose."
   1. English Language—Rime—Juvenile literature.
[1. English language—Rime] I. Title.
PE1517.C5   398.8   77-20994
ISBN 0-516-03629-7

Copyright © 1978 by Regensteiner Publishing Enterprises, Inc.
All rights reserved. Published simultaneously in Canada.
Printed in the United States of America.

    6 7 8 9 10 11 12 R 85 84 83 82 81

Calico Cat and Shaggy Dog
have a good time
trying to think
of words that rhyme.

"There's a frog on my log," said Shaggy Dog.

"There's a rat
in my hat,"
said Calico Cat.

"There's a bee on my knee."

"There's a snail on my tail."

"There's a fish in my dish."

"There's a rose on my nose."

"There's a chair in my hair."

"There's a bed
on my head."

"There's a goat in my boat."

"There's a dragon in our wagon!"

Calico Cat and Shaggy Dog can make words rhyme.

Can you?

Bug in a _____.
Bee in a _____.
Mouse in a _____.
Snake in a _____.
Bear in a _____.

ABOUT THE AUTHOR/ARTIST

Donald Charles started his long career as an artist and author more than twenty-five years ago after attending the University of California and the Art League School of California. He began by writing and illustrating feature articles for the *San Francisco Chronicle,* and also sold cartoons and ideas to *The New Yorker* and *Cosmopolitan* magazines. Since then he has been, at various times, a longshoreman, ranch hand, truck driver, and editor of a weekly newspaper, all enriching experiences for a writer and artist. Ultimately he became creative director for an advertising agency, a post which he resigned several years ago to devote himself full-time to book illustration and writing. Mr. Charles has received frequent awards from graphic societies, and his work has appeared in numerous textbooks and periodicals.